D1256057

Birds CAn Fly, Why Can't I?

Written by
Vicki Addesso Dodd
& David Hill

Illustrated by
David Hill

The illustrations in this book are oil paintings on panel inspired by LOVE.

ISBN-10: 0990337355
ISBN-13: 978-0990337355
Text copyright c2015 Vicki Addesso Dodd
Illustration copyright c2015 David Hill

Published in 2015 by
Saratoga Springs Publishing, L.L.C.
P.O.Box 102
Saratoga Springs, NY
SaratogaSpringsPublishing@gmail.com
www.SaratogaSpringsPublishing.com

Created and Illustrated by David Hill
www.DavidHillGallery@hotmail.com
www.DavidHillGallery.com

Production Design by Patrick Jankowski
www.jankdesign.com

Text editing by
Briana Kuruzovich
brianabk@yahoo.com

Saratoga Springs Publishing's books are available at special discounts when purchased
in quantity for premiums and promotions as well as fundraising or educational use.
Special editions can also be created to specification.

For details or to purchase any of our products
please contact us at:

www.SaratogaSpringsPublishing.com

To my dear Griffin, I created this book for you. You were my motivation, my inspiration and my wonder. As you grow, always remember that you have the ability to defy gravity while chasing your dreams. ~ DH

For my amazing daughter, Kelsey, who always continues to make me proud. When I grow up I want to be just like you!
And to David, thank you for sharing your dream with me. ~ VAD

Oh, I wish that I could fly
like the birds up in the sky.

All the places that I'd see
with my friends beside of me.

We'd scale the mountaintops
together.

But I have no wings,
not even a feather.

Are wings the only way to fly?

There must be other
ways to try........

The wind may carry up my kite,

but sticks and cloth won't
help my flight.

Wait! My plane has wings
that fly.

It circles trees it passes by.

A toy airplane
may take me there.

Do they build one
that carries a bear?

A real airplane could be
the one

to fly me past the clouds
and sun.

But a ticket to the sky

is much more than this
bear can buy.

Superheroes seem to fly.

It's kind of scary but
worth a try.

But a super cape just can't be found,

that gets this panda
off the ground.

I guess this bear cannot take flight.

I'll close my eyes and say good night.

As I sleep I start to see....

my bed move far
away from me!

I see the clouds.

I feel the sun.

I'm flying with the birds
as one!

As an airplane passes me,

I say, "Let's race".....
1.....2.....3!

Wait, I see my house again.

I think my flight's
about to end.

What a night!

It seemed so real,

to see these places
I can't feel.

I now know how it feels to fly,
to soar through clouds
as birds pass by.

No wings or feathers for this bear.
My dreams at night
will take me there.

I hope I have that dream

tonight.........

Sweet dreams and
have a happy flight.

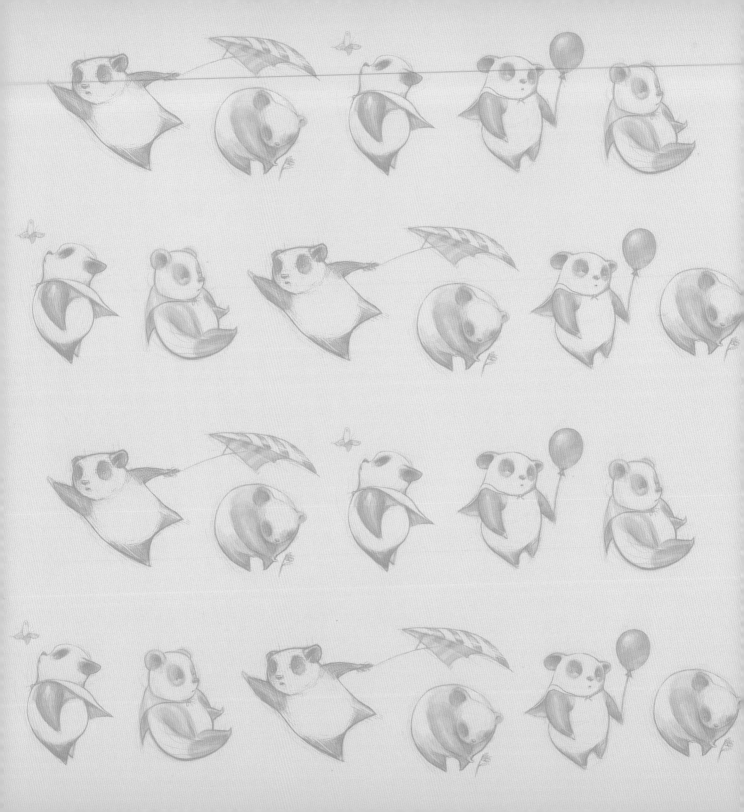

Vicki Addesso Dodd is the award winning children's book author of the popular children's books *I Love You Daddy, I Love You More, A Moose in My Stable* and *A Pumpkin for a Princess*. Born and raised in New Jersey, she now lives in historic Saratoga Springs with her family and two best friends, her husband, Gregg, and daughter, Kelsey. Together, along with their two furry friends, they create beautiful stories and inspiration. Vicki loves to hear from her readers. You can contact her on Facebook - Saratoga Springs Publishing or visit her online at www.SaratogaSpringsPublishing.com

David Hill is a well known and highly collected Caribbean artist from the Virgin Islands. After years of enduring island beaches and sun while developing his artistic name he moved to Saratoga, New York, with his wife Emily, son Griffin, daughter Bea, and cats: Vincent and Jengo.

Working with galleries in New York, New Jersey, Connecticut, and Maine, David has expanded his following and artistic possibilities. With new landscapes there comes new endeavors, new people to work with, and new creations. More of David's work can be viewed at www.davidhillgallery.com